Zoe Gentleman was born and raised in Essex, England, in 1989. Upon leaving school, Zoe was employed in an administrative role at a legal firm in the heart of London.

She is married and has a beautiful young daughter, who ultimately inspired her to write this unique and heartfelt story.

Nellie's ROARSOME Adventure

Zoe Gentleman

Austin Macauley Publishers™
LONDON • CAMBRIDGE • NEW YORK • SHARJAH

www.austinmacauley.com

First Published (2020)
Austin Macauley Publishers Ltd
25 Canada Square
Canary Wharf
London
E14 5LQ

For Nellie, who brought the dinosaurs into our world.

Thank you to my darling husband and family for always encouraging me to aim high.

Nellie is playing in the garden with her best friend, Bunny; her mummy is watering some flowers when out of nowhere she hears loud stomping.

She slowly turns her head and sees a herd of diplodocus walking in front of her. They are her favourite dinosaur because they are SO BIG. "Wow, did you see that, Bunny? Let's go and explore!" shouts Nellie.

She runs to catch up with them, stretching her hand out to touch their bumpy skin.

Nellie stops and turns around in a circle and appears to have entered a magical Jurassic jungle. She can see streaming waterfalls and lakes, which are surrounded by colourful flowers and the biggest trees that she has ever seen. "This place is beautiful," says Nellie.

Nellie hears a noise; she looks around and finds a little baby diplodocus crying. "What's wrong?" Nellie asks.

"I can't find my mummy," the dinosaur replies.

"Don't worry, we will find her... What is your name?" Nellie asks.

The dinosaur lifts her long neck up and looks at Nellie.

"My name is Bella," the dinosaur replies.

"Hi Bella, I am Nellie, and this is Bunny. So what does your mummy like to do?" Nellie asks. Bella has a moment to think.

"She likes to have a drink by the lake," says Bella.

"Then that's where we should go," says Nellie. Side by side, Nellie and Bella walk towards the lake.

Bella leads the way, with Nellie walking behind. Nellie looks up to the sky, and she can't believe what she can see. Above her head are a family of pterodactyls, flying and diving through the sky. Their wings are making the leaves in the trees shake! "Wow," whispers Nellie.

As they approach the lake, she has to wave her hand in front of her face to keep the enormous dragonflies at bay. "It's so pretty," says Nellie. There are dinosaurs all around her, drinking at the lake.

They both take a look around. "Is your mummy here?" Nellie asks.

Bella shakes her long neck and sighs, "No, she's not here; she has an extra big pointy spike on her back, and I can't see that on any of these dinosaurs," said Bella.

"Oh okay, don't worry, Bella. What else does your mummy like to do?" Nellie asks.

"She likes to rest by the palm trees just past the river," says Bella.

"Then that's where we should go," says Nellie.

Nellie and Bella set off when they spot a very LARGE T-REX!!! Nellie and Bella hide behind a bush. "Oh no, a T-Rex, be very quiet, Bella. We don't want the T-Rex to hear us!" Nellie whispers. They both stay down, Nellie cuddling Bunny close to her. The T-Rex lowers her head towards them, and she starts to sniff Nellie's hair.

"No need to be frightened, I'm not going to hurt you. What are you two little girls doing out here, all by yourselves?" the big friendly T-Rex asks.

Nellie stood up tall.

"We are looking for Bella's mummy, have you seen her?" Nellie asks.

"Yes, yes, I have. She is by the palm trees, looking for you, Bella. Follow me, and I will take you to her," says the T-Rex.

Nellie couldn't have been more excited. A T-Rex wants to help them, and she is lovely—not at all scary! Nellie trying to stomp like a T-Rex walks alongside her dinosaur friends.

Walking through trees, trees and more trees, Nellie spots a very big dinosaur in the distance, stomping through the palm trees.

"Is that your mummy over there?" Nellie asks excitedly.

"Yes, yes. She is over there," pointing to a very large diplodocus with an extra big pointy spike on her back just like Bella had mentioned.

Bella and Nellie run over to Bella's mummy, with the T-Rex not far behind.

Bella's mum wraps her long neck around Bella. "Thank you, Nellie, for helping me find my mummy," says Bella.

"You're welcome, Bella. I have had the BEST day ever, but I best get back to my mummy!" Nellie laughs.

Nellie gives Bella a big cuddle and they say their goodbyes. "Follow me, Nellie, I will guide you home," says the T-Rex and with a quick walk, Nellie can see her garden in front of her. Nellie gives the T-Rex a big squeeze and says, "Thank you for showing me home."

"You're welcome, Nellie, have a ROARSOME day!!!" roars the T-Rex.

As Nellie and Bunny walk back into her garden, she can see her mummy watering the same flowers. *Time must have stayed still*, she thought. As she looks behind her, the Jurassic jungle begins fading into the distance. She smiles and hopes she will see it again. She runs to her mummy and says, "Mummy, Mummy, I have just had the most ROARSOME adventure ever."